To E.G., my newest hero

Special thanks to Benjamin Scott

Bloomsbury Publishing, London, New Delhi, New York and Sydney

First published in Great Britain in August 2012 by Bloomsbury Publishing Plc
50 Bedford Square, London, WC1B 3DP

Text copyright © Working Partners 2012
Illustrations copyright © Sam Hadley 2012

The moral rights of the author and illustrator have been asserted

A CIP catalogue record for this book is available from the British Library

ISBN 978 1 4088 2716 1

Typeset by Hewer Text UK Ltd, Edinburgh
Printed in Great Britain by Clays Ltd, St Ives plc, Bungay, Suffolk

1 3 5 7 9 10 8 6 4 2

www.bloomsbury.com
www.starfighterbooks.com

MAX CHASE

Illustrated by Sam Hadley

BLOOMSBURY

LONDON   NEW DELHI   NEW YORK   SYDNEY

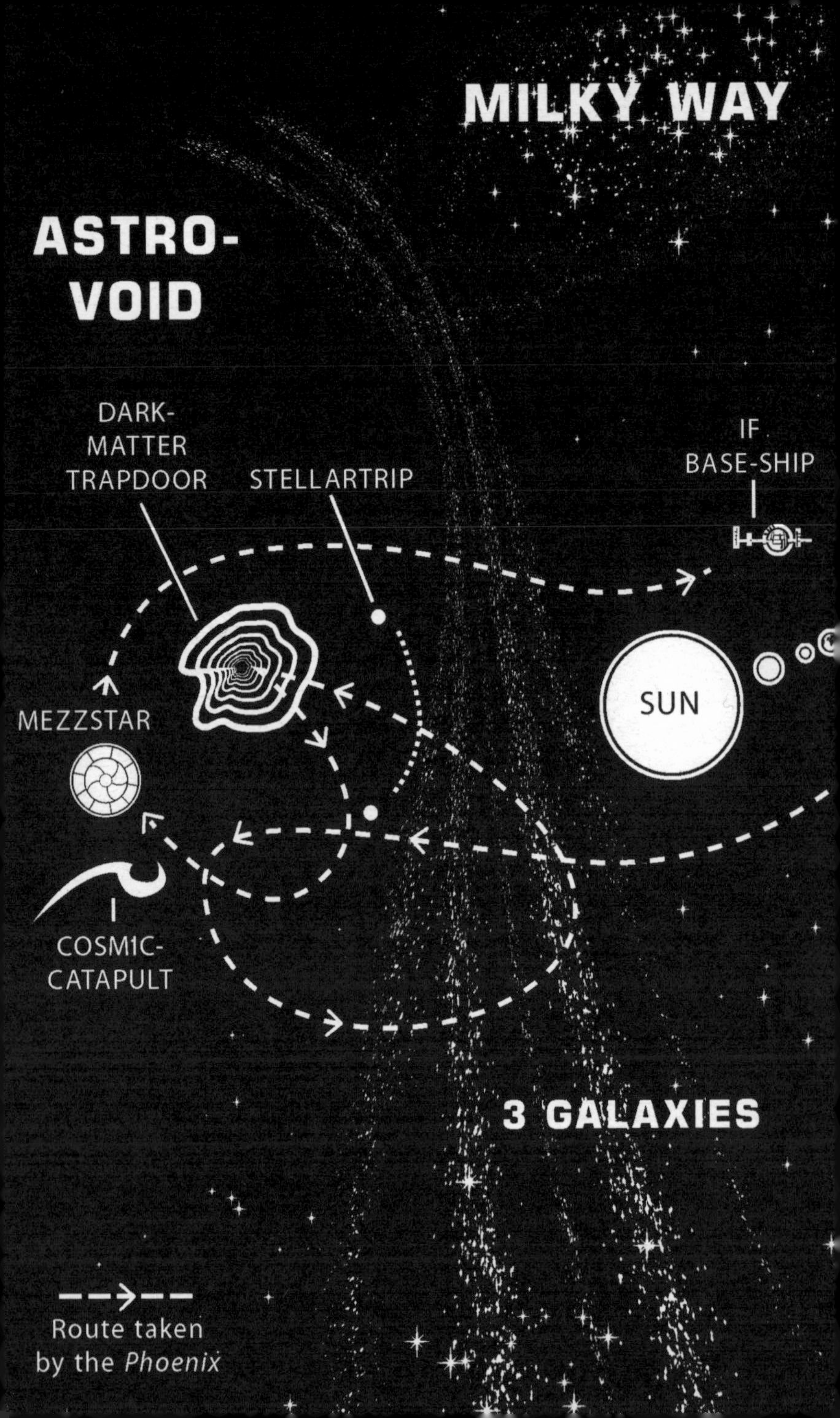
MILKY WAY
ASTRO-
VOID
DARK-
MATTER
TRAPDOOR
STELLARTRIP
IF
BASE-SHIP
MEZZSTAR
SUN
COSMIC-
CATAPULT
3 GALAXIES
Route taken
by the *Phoenix*

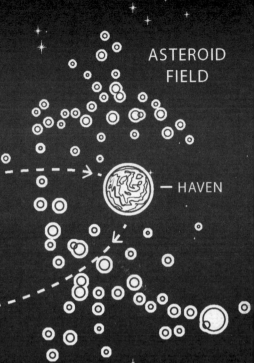

ASTEROID
FIELD

— HAVEN

**RUMANA
GALAXY**

7 GALAXIES

STAR FIGHTERS

An elite fighting team sworn to protect and defend the galaxy

It is the year 5012 and the Milky Way galaxy is under attack . . .

After the Universal War . . . a war that almost brought about the destruction of every known universe . . . the planets in the Milky Way banded together to create the Intergalactic Force – an elite fighting team sworn to protect and defend the galaxy.

Only the brightest and most promising students are accepted into the Intergalactic Force Academy, and only the very best cadets reach the highest of their ranks and become . . .

To be a Star Fighter is to dedicate your life to one mission: *Peace in Space*. They are given the coolest weapons, the fastest spaceships – and the most dangerous missions. Everyone at the Intergalactic Force Academy wants to be a Star Fighter someday.

Do YOU have what it takes?

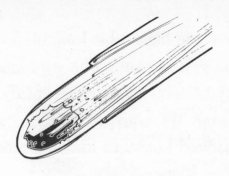

Chapter 1

'Wow!' Peri gasped. Through the 360-monitor, he could see a comet whooshing through outer space like an old-fashioned firework – the kind he had seen in *Did They Really Do That?*, a film about ancient Earth customs. The comet was going to miss the *Phoenix* by only a few hundred kilometres.

'We don't have time to admire the scenery, you voidoid,' Diesel said. 'Have you forgotten our mission? We have to recover the Heart of Mars.'

'And then hand over this criminal!' Otto

grunted. He flicked his long black tongue in Jaxx's direction. Their official Star Fighter mission was to capture the space pirate, but the emperor had also secretly commanded Diesel to find and return the Heart of Mars.

Selene moved closer to Jaxx, her father. 'He's no pirate!'

'That's right, I'm not,' Jaxx said. His voice was mild, polite, friendly – the exact opposite of how Peri imagined a space pirate would sound.

Jaxx had escaped from prison and Peri and the crew of the *Phoenix* had finally chased him down in the rings of Saturn. They had rescued him from his stealth ship only a nanosecond before it blew up, and then arrested him. Only Selene's pleading had spared him from being turned in to the Intergalactic Force immediately.

Jaxx held out his hands. 'Perhaps you could take these handcuffs off me now?'

'We did agree to trust him,' Peri said, as he saw Otto eyeing Jaxx suspiciously.

'*I* didn't!' Otto boomed.

'Come on! He is our friend's dad,' Peri said. He touched a section of the wall and the Bits and Bobs drawer slid out. He pulled out the Universal Release Gun and pointed it at Jaxx's wrists. There was a sizzling sound and the handcuffs melted into a silvery goo that dripped on the floor of the Bridge.

'Hey!' Otto protested. 'Those handcuffs are my property!'

'*Were y*our property,' Selene said with a grin.

'Thanks,' Jaxx said, shaking the goo from his hands.

'So, you say you know where the Heart of Mars is?' Diesel demanded.

The Heart of Mars was a priceless, glowing, orange orb of pure chrysolite from Mars, the size of a Meigwor's fist. It belonged to the Martian royal family. Diesel's father, the emperor, believed that all Martians would be cursed until the Heart of Mars was returned.

'I don't know for sure where it is,' Jaxx said. When Diesel's yellow eyes narrowed in disbelief, he quickly followed up with, 'But I do have a pretty good idea where to look.'

'Where, then?' Diesel pressed.

Jaxx pointed out of the 360-monitor. 'In that beautiful comet,' he said.

'That's the comet you plotted a course for, back on Haven?' Peri said.

Jaxx nodded. 'It's two years since the comet last passed through the Milky Way, and it's also two years since the Heart of Mars was stolen.'

Peri saw Diesel's fists clench. 'That doesn't prove anything!' Diesel shouted.

'I know,' Jaxx said. 'But I have strong reason to believe that . . . Well, just take it from me, the jewel is on that comet.'

'And who put it there, Mr Space-Pirate-Who-Says-He-Isn't-A-Space-Pirate?' boomed Otto. 'If it wasn't you, then who was it?'

'Just . . . someone I know.'

Peri felt a tingle of dread in his circuits. Jaxx didn't seem as relaxed as before. He was acting as if he was trying to hide something. Perhaps he wasn't as innocent as he'd claimed?

'Leave him alone!' Selene snapped, squaring up to Otto. 'My dad didn't steal anything — but he knows who did and he knows where the gem is. Isn't that enough?'

'What if it's not really there?' Diesel objected. 'We will have wasted even more time.'

Peri had an idea. 'The Heart of Mars has a constant temperature, doesn't it?' he asked Diesel.

Diesel nodded. 'It's what they call a warm-blooded stone. If you put it in a freezer, it gets no colder. Put it in a furnace and it gets no hotter.'

'Right,' Peri said. 'So the comet, travelling through deep space, must be pretty close to absolute zero. We just need to do a heat-scan – if a warm spot shows up, we know it's the Heart of Mars.'

'Brilliant!' Selene said.

Peri clicked his fingers. The control panel glided across the Bridge towards him. His special connection to the *Phoenix* meant that he knew instinctively what to do. His fingers moved rapidly over the console as he activated the infrared scanner.

An image of the comet appeared on the monitor. The body was a uniform dull red.

'That can't be right,' Peri said. 'It looks like the whole thing's warm.'

'Maybe the Heart of Mars heated the comet up,' Selene suggested.

Diesel shook his head. 'It's far too small to warm up a whole comet.'

'It's weird,' Peri said slowly. 'I wonder if the scanner's not working properly.'

'Whatever your instruments tell you,' Jaxx said, 'the Heart of Mars has to be on that comet. Trust me.'

'That's just the trouble,' Otto grunted. 'We don't.'

Selene glared at Otto. 'The only thing we can do is land on the comet and look for the stone ourselves. When we find it, that'll prove my dad is innocent.'

Peri didn't see how this would prove Jaxx's innocence – especially since Jaxx had been planning to intercept the comet before the *Phoenix* came along. He didn't say any of this aloud though. It would only upset Selene. Besides, right now the important thing was to recover the stone, whoever had stolen it.

'We've got to try,' Peri said. He had to

prove General Pegg wrong. The general had made it clear that he wasn't sure if Peri and Diesel were cut out to be Star Fighters.

'The comet is very small,' said Jaxx. 'You won't be able to land the *Phoenix* on it. And it's travelling towards us at about fifty kilometres a second,' he added. 'It's going to be very difficult to land anything at all.'

'Well, we'll think of a way,' Peri said. He wasn't about to fail — not when his future as a Star Fighter depended on it. 'We've just got to.'

Chapter 2

'There must be a way to do this,' Peri said. 'Jaxx, how were you planning to intercept the comet?'

'I had a one-person stealth craft – it was small enough to land on the surface,' Jaxx replied.

'Couldn't we just shrink the *Phoenix*?' suggested Selene.

'Not when it's in motion,' Peri said.

'Even if you *had* landed on the comet,' Diesel said to Jaxx, 'how were you going to look for such a small stone?'

X-Ray Detector,'
behind when you
alth craft.'
said. 'The *Phoenix*
ay Detector too.'
o fly very close and
distance to get a good
reading,' Jaxx said.

Otto yawned noisily. 'Boring!' he said. 'There's no way we can search that comet, so it's a waste of time talking about it.' He yawned again and stretched, flexing his long rubbery arms.

'Wait a minute,' said Diesel, staring at Otto's limbs. 'What about a laser lasso! If we let the comet pull us along, we'd maintain the same speed.'

'That might work,' Peri said, slapping Diesel on the back. Maybe they were finally beginning to work as a team.

'Yes,' Jaxx said. His whole manner changed. He seemed to take control of the Bridge. 'Peri, if Selene and I plot the coordinates, can you pilot the ship and bring it in close? And, Diesel, can you fire the lasso?'

'What about me?' Otto grumbled. 'What am I supposed to do?'

Jaxx shrugged. 'Try not to get in the way.'

Peri sat down in the captain's chair and took hold of the ship's Nav-wheel, as Otto moved to the back of the Bridge. Peri glanced across at Selene and her dad standing together, bent over a computer screen. The family resemblance between them was obvious now. He wondered how he hadn't noticed it when he first saw the images of Jaxx on the Mission Capsule.

'Sixteen degrees starboard,' Jaxx called out. 'And ten degrees under.'

Peri twisted the Nav-wheel to the right

and downwards. On the 360-monitor, he saw the comet growing in size as it approached.

'Hold starboard course,' Jaxx said. 'Another two degrees under.'

Peri tilted the Nav-wheel.

'Diesel, get ready,' said Selene. Diesel was sitting at the gunnery station, hands poised over the controls. 'Ten, nine, eight . . .'

The comet was rushing up to meet them. *If we hit it at this speed*, Peri thought, *we'll be smashed to pieces!*

'Correct the course!' Jaxx said. 'Five degrees to port.'

Peri corrected. The comet now appeared at a slight angle to them. Peri could see it clearly. A large coppery shape, like a flattened ball, covered in spiky humps and bumps, the sparkling tail streaming behind it.

'. . . three, two, one – fire!'

Diesel hit the firing button. Peri saw a golden rope fly out from the *Phoenix*, encircle the body of the comet and draw itself tight. He felt a slight tug on the ship as the laser rope took the strain. The *Phoenix* shifted course slightly. They were now being towed along by the comet.

'Nice work!' Jaxx said. He and Selene high-fived each other.

'Are we close enough to use the Detector now?' Peri asked.

'For sure,' Jaxx said. 'The laser lasso keeps us within range.'

Diesel emerged from the gunnery station. Peri could tell Diesel was very pleased with himself. His strip of hair glowed bright yellow. 'Good idea of mine, wasn't it?'

'Ten out of ten,' Jaxx said. 'Now let's get the Detector on the case.'

Peri clicked his fingers again, and the

control panel floated over to him. He swiftly found the programme for the Detector.

A sharp, stern woman's voice echoed around the Bridge: *'HELLO. I AM THE ELEMENTAL X-RAY DETECTOR.'*

'Wow,' Jaxx said. 'State of the art. My El-X-Ray Detector didn't speak to me.'

'PLEASE DO NOT CALL ME THE "EL-X-RAY". I DISLIKE IT.'

Peri saw Jaxx smile.

'PLEASE ENTER THE COORDINATES FOR YOUR DESIGNATED SCAN-ZONE.'

Peri wished it had a nicer voice. It reminded him of Mrs Zargonara, the hyper-strict maths teacher at the IF Academy.

'PLEASE ENTER THE COORDINATES!' the voice said. *'I HAVE ASKED YOU ONCE ALREADY.'*

'What are the coordinates?' Peri asked Jaxx.

'Relative to *Phoenix*, 28 starboard, 11 under, distance 0.0000000000571 of a parsec, velocity zero.'

'You got it!' Peri was tapping in the numbers as Jaxx spoke. A close-up of the comet filled the 360-monitor.

'*SCAN-ZONE FOUND*,' said the programme. '*ENTER YOUR SEARCH TERMS.*'

Peri keyed in *MARTIAN CHRYSOLITE*.

The image on the monitor remained unchanged.

'*NO RESULTS MATCHING YOUR SEARCH TERMS. ARE YOU SURE YOU HAVE SPELT IT CORRECTLY? CHECK YOUR SEARCH TERMS AND RE-ENTER.*'

The programme sounded annoyed that they had made a mistake. Peri felt a hot tingle in his wiring, the way he had in Mrs Zargonara's maths class when he got an answer wrong.

Diesel's strip of hair had turned a crestfallen brown. Selene looked devastated. She gazed up at her dad, as if waiting for a word of consolation or explanation.

'*I ASKED YOU TO CHECK YOUR SEARCH TERMS,*' the computer programme said irritably. '*I HAVEN'T GOT ALL DAY!*'

'I don't understand,' Jaxx muttered.

'I do!' boomed Otto, walking back to the front of the Bridge. 'You just made up the story about the Heart of Mars so that we wouldn't turn you in! You can't fool a Meigwor!'

'Wait,' said Peri. 'Could the Heart be inside a protective box or case?'

Jaxx's face lit up. So did Selene's. 'Lead,' she cried. 'X-rays can't see through lead. Maybe the Heart is inside something made of lead.'

Peri keyed in the word *LEAD*.

'*ABOUT TIME*,' the programme said. '*LET'S HOPE WE HAVE MORE LUCK WITH THIS ONE ... YES, RESULT FOUND. IT WOULD HAVE SAVED TIME HAD YOU ENTERED IT CORRECTLY TO BEGIN WITH.*'

'Oh, be quiet,' Peri muttered. He'd always wanted to say that to Mrs Zargonara. He turned the volume down to zero before the programme could answer back.

On the 360-monitor Peri saw a small dot that hadn't been there before. He used the touchpad to zoom in on it. It showed up as a black, cylindrical object.

'Yes!' Selene shouted.

'The Heart must be inside that container,' Jaxx said. 'Well done, Peri!'

'How do you know there's anything inside it?' Otto said. 'It could be empty. You still haven't proved anything!'

'We have no choice — we'll have to land and check it out,' Peri said.

'What's that?' Selene said, her voice suddenly urgent.

'Oh my . . .' Jaxx said.

Peri looked up. He could hardly believe his eyes. Two huge pincers had sprung from the body of the comet like cosmic crab claws. They snapped threateningly.

The comet was alive!

The claws loomed larger on the monitor as they moved towards the *Phoenix*.

'Aaagh!' Otto squealed.

Diesel's strip of hair turned a terrified grey.

One claw snipped right through the laser lasso. Peri felt the slight jerk as the *Phoenix* broke free.

The other claw swiped towards the ship. Peri grabbed the Nav-wheel, but he was too late.

The impact sent a shudder through the *Phoenix*, and the crew fell, sprawling across the floor.

The 360-monitor filled with a whirling pattern of blackness and stars, then a jumble of silvery rocks and dust as the *Phoenix* tumbled headlong into the tail of the comet.

Chapter 3

Huge rocks from the comet's tail crashed against the *Phoenix*.

'*Ach' baxbr!*' Diesel cried, as the ship was knocked crazily from left to right.

The crew were hurled back and forth across the Bridge. Peri's hands flew across the control panel as he switched on the shield. But even that did nothing to stop the ship from shaking with each new impact. He grabbed the Nav-wheel and pulled hard away from the comet.

Finally the *Phoenix* was clear of the debris.

The stars stopped spinning. They were safe but the comet zoomed away from them, its claws still snapping at outer space.

Diesel drew a deep breath. 'That thing is fast!'

'Can the *Phoenix* catch up with it?' Jaxx asked.

'This ship can catch anything,' Peri said. 'But I'm not sure I want to catch *that!*'

'Let's follow it at a safe distance,' Selene suggested, 'until we find out what it is.'

'OK,' Peri said. He turned the Nav-wheel and engaged the thrusters. The comet – or whatever it was – grew larger as the *Phoenix* got closer. 'Let's check it out in the *Space Spotter's Guide.*' On Peri's command, an InfoBox appeared:

Space Spotter's Guide

A comprehensive guide to the universe, including all 19,756,890, 089,390,111,548,333,891 known life forms.

'There are so many,' Diesel said. 'How are we going to figure out what this thing is?'

'Yeah, I bet there are thousands of species of copper-coloured life forms the size of spaceships that whizz through space like comets and have giant claws,' Peri said.

'There won't be thousands, you dumb-oid!' Diesel said.

Martians don't really get sarcasm, Peri thought.

'Come on, Peri,' Selene snapped. 'We haven't got time for this. Just find out what that thing is!'

Peri typed in the 'Observed features' of the life form he wished to search for. A picture of the copper-coloured 'comet' with protruding claws appeared on the 360-monitor. Below it was an InfoBox:

Trojan Crab

DESCRIPTION: Giant space crustacean of the genus Cancridae astronomicus. The Trojan Crab may grow up to half a kilometre across and its gravity is powerful enough to attract a 'tail' of rocks and space dust. It travels through space utilising the solar wind from stars. Omnivorous. No reported sightings within the last 1,000 years. Possibly extinct.

HAZARDS: The Trojan Crab can be dangerous if provoked.

'That's why everyone thought it was a comet,' Jaxx said.

'Let's get a bit closer,' said Peri. 'I want to have a better look.'

Peri eased the *Phoenix* forward. The

Trojan Crab loomed up in the 360-monitor. An eye on a stalk popped out and swivelled round until it spotted the *Phoenix*. Then its massive claw swung their way again.

Peri jerked the Nav-wheel. The giant claw missed. But only just.

'Let's get out of here!' Otto boomed. 'We've completed our mission – we've captured Jaxx.'

'No – we have to find the Heart of Mars!' Diesel said.

'If only there was a way to get close and search it,' Selene said.

'What about the rocket packs?' Peri asked. 'We could jet down and land on the comet – um, I mean crab.'

'Are you crazy?' Otto shouted. 'You want to land on a giant, flying crab-comet?'

'We'll be fine,' Peri said.

'Well, *I* will be,' Otto said. 'Because I'm staying right here.'

'A one-man rocket is probably too small for it to notice,' Peri said. 'Plus, we'll be wearing the rocket packs – if we need to, we can jet out of trouble!'

Peri was starting to feel excited. He had always wanted to use the rocket packs. He wished, though, that they had been trained to use them at the IF Academy. Trying them out for the first time while landing on a humongous Trojan Crab zooming through space was not going to be easy.

It was going to be ultra-dangerous.

'I'm up for it!' said Diesel. 'I'll do anything to get the Heart of Mars back.'

'I'll come too,' Jaxx said.

Otto's long crimson arm coiled round Jaxx's neck. 'No you won't!' he boomed.

'You are still our prisoner and I'm not letting you out of my sight.'

Selene took a step towards him. 'Get off him, or I'll –'

Otto stuck his long neck out so his face was close to hers. 'Or you'll what?'

'I'll set the ship's thermostat to zero degrees,' Selene said.

Otto's eyes widened. The Meigwor hated cold temperatures. 'No need for that,' he said. He removed his arm from round Jaxx's neck, but remained standing close to him.

'I'd better stay behind,' Selene said, 'so that I can make sure this freak doesn't do anything stupid.'

Jaxx gave Otto an angry look and moved away from him. 'You'll need a portable Elemental X-Ray Detector,' he said to Peri. 'Let's see what we can rig up. Is there a workshop on this ship?'

Peri pulled out the Bits and Bobs drawer from the wall again. 'You'll probably find what you need in here,' he said.

Jaxx sorted out a heap of junk and spread it on the floor. 'Let's see, this bit of tungsten will come in handy, and this biotic battery, and this length of spectro-cable, and this Moebius strip . . .'

Selene, who loved messing about with

gadgets, leaned over his shoulder and was soon helping him put it all together. In a couple of minutes they'd rigged up a strange box. It had various rods sticking out like little arms, a miniature screen and a sort of funnel on top. Selene plugged it into the ship's computer.

Download Complete, flashed on to the machine's screen less than a minute later.

'It's ready,' Jaxx said. 'This will use the Elemental X-Ray Detector programme from your computer. I'm afraid this one won't speak to you though.'

'Good!' Peri smiled at Jaxx. 'Ready?' he said.

'Ready,' Diesel replied.

They stood in the *Phoenix*'s air-lock, in their Expedition Wear, with the rocket packs strapped on. Peri held the Detector. Around his shoulders Diesel was wearing a garish flag with red, green, yellow, blue, orange and turquoise stripes. The flag of Mars. It was made of Bio-Cloth, and the colours shimmered and moved.

'Do you have to wear that thing?' Peri said. 'I get a headache just looking at it.'

'Of course I have to wear it,' Diesel said. 'I'm a royal prince on a mission to recover the Heart of Mars – obviously I have to wear the flag of Mars!'

'Suit yourself,' Peri muttered.

'Well, what are we waiting for?' Diesel said.

'Open outer portal,' Peri commanded.

The outer air-lock door obediently slid open.

'Let's see what this baby can do,' Peri said, touching the control of the rocket pack.

The next thing he knew, he was whooshing through the air-lock and jetting through space.

Wow! The sense of freedom was incredible.

A moment later, Diesel appeared beside him, somersaulting over and over.

Peri heard Diesel's voice in his ear, through the Expedition Wear's com-unit. 'Difficult to control, aren't they?'

Peri crashed into him. 'We'll soon get the hang of it.'

They were both attached to the *Phoenix* by long, flexible, steel safety cables.

The hand-held rocket pack control was circular, with six arrows on it. One for up, one for down, one left, one right, one forwards, one backwards.

'You'll have to use your rockets to power forward,' Peri yelled.

'I got it,' Diesel called as he zoomed past Peri.

It took some getting used to, but soon both Peri and Diesel had the controls figured out. Peri felt incredibly light and free. *It's just like in those dreams where you can fly,* he thought, *except at supersonic velocity.*

'Punch the rocket pulse button for a burst of speed,' Peri told Diesel. 'We need to jet ahead and catch that crab!'

Soon the copper-coloured shell of the Trojan Crab was below their feet.

'Time to touch down!' Peri called to Diesel.

They zoomed down and landed with a double thump on the Crab's shell. Up close, it was obviously a living creature. The shell was covered with bumps and scars, and parasitic space-insects scuttled around on it.

'Pass me that X-ray thing,' Diesel said. He started clomping over the shell, sweeping around with the portable Elemental X-Ray Detector.

'Careful!' said Peri. 'We don't want it to know that we're here. It's omnivorous, remember?'

'I meant to ask you about that,' Diesel said. 'What does "omnivorous" mean?'

'It means it eats everything.'

Diesel's hair started to turn white. *'Everything?'*

The ground beneath their feet began to tremble and quake before two eyes on stalks popped up from the edge of the shell. With a metallic whine, they swivelled round to stare at Peri and Diesel.

'I think the Crab knows we're here,' Peri said.

Chapter 4

Eight pincers on long, flexible arms popped out from around the sides of the Trojan Crab and snaked their way towards Peri and Diesel.

'*Krawbanoxbazong!*' Diesel screamed.

Peri jabbed the 'Up' arrow on the rocket pack control. He felt a snapping pincer just brush his heels as he rose.

Already another pincer was coming for him. This one looked big enough to chop him in half.

He jabbed the 'Back' arrow. The pincer slammed shut centimetres from his face.

Every time I dodge one claw, I fall into the path of another one, he thought. *I don't know how long I can keep this up!*

Diesel was frantically dodging the claws too. The shimmering, colourful Martian flag fluttered from his shoulders like a cape as he swooped left and right. The claws seemed to follow him hungrily. The Trojan Crab now seemed much more interested in Diesel than in Peri.

'Let's get out of here!' Peri shouted.

'No!' Diesel's voice crackled into Peri's earpiece. 'I'm not giving up now we're this close to the Heart of Mars!' He zoomed towards the creature. 'I'm taking a closer look.' He held the Elemental X-Ray Detector in front of him like a sword and charged towards the shell. A claw whipped in from the side and chomped clean through Diesel's rocket pack. He pressed frantically on his hand-held control, but nothing happened. Another claw swayed towards him, pincers snapping.

'Diesel!' Peri shouted. 'Grab the safety cable – pull yourself clear!'

A second later, Peri had to jet away from a deadly claw himself.

Diesel seized the cable that attached him to the *Phoenix* and started to climb up it hand over hand.

Thrum-thwack! A crab claw sliced through the safety harness and latched on to Diesel.

'Nooooo!' Diesel yelled. His arms and legs waved wildly, but he wasn't going anywhere.

Peri zoomed towards him. They would have to forget about the Heart of Mars. He needed to save his friend and take him back to the ship.

Before Peri reached Diesel, the Trojan

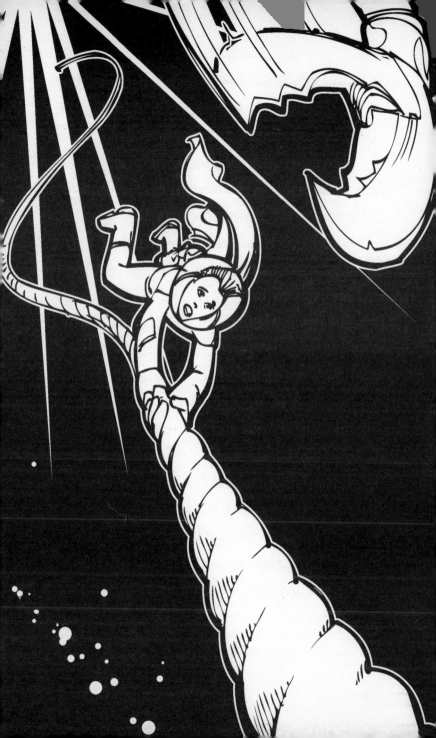

Crab lashed at him with another claw. The blow sent Peri hurtling head over heels into space.

'What's happening down there?' Otto's voice boomed in Peri's earpiece. 'Looks like you're having problems!'

'A few,' Peri said, still somersaulting.

'I'll save you,' Otto said, 'by blasting the Crab with the laser cannon.'

'No!' Peri said. 'You might hit Diesel.'

'True,' Otto agreed, and Peri thought he could hear a smile in the Meigwor's voice. 'Let's risk it!'

'Stay away from that laser cannon!' Peri commanded.

In the background he heard Selene say, 'Don't touch it, Otto!'

Peri finally managed to stop spinning. He ignored the queasy feeling in his stomach as he looked down to see how Diesel was doing. Peri felt a stab of fear, as if his heart had slammed on the brakes.

Diesel was clamped tight in the Crab's pincer. His hands were braced against the claw as he tried to tug himself out, and his legs kicked wildly.

There wasn't a moment to lose. That giant pincer could chop Diesel in half if the Crab exerted a little more pressure. Peri drew his phaser, but, before he could fire, the Crab released Diesel, and tossed him up into space.

'*Bleukenzzaminosh!*' Diesel shouted as he flew in a low, looping curve all the way across the shell. When he reached the other side, another claw arose and gently batted him back the way he had come. Then the first claw popped up again and knocked him back the other way. The creature's stalky eyes widened as they followed

Diesel's progress back and forth, like a spectator at a tennis match.

'What the *blooblazeez* is it doing?' Diesel howled.

'I think it's playing with you,' Peri said.

Diesel managed to draw his phaser in mid-flight. 'I don't want to play!' he yelled as he blasted an energy ray at the Crab's shell. The ray crackled and fizzed as it bounced off the Crab's shell. Even on the 'Standard' setting this would have been enough to bring an elephant to its knees. But it seemed to have no effect at all on the Trojan Crab.

Peri jetted over to Diesel. When he was almost within reach, the Crab sent Diesel whirling through space again. Peri turned and zoomed after his friend, but he had barely got halfway when Diesel was sent tumbling in the other direction.

This is a cosmic game of piggy in the middle, Peri fumed.

'Help me!' Diesel shouted.

'I'm trying!'

Again, Peri jetted after Diesel. But now the Crab seemed to have tired of the game. It gripped Diesel in its pincer once again and carried him firmly to the front of the shell, where its eyes were.

Peri's blood turned to ice. *Its mouth must be there too!* The Trojan Crab had been playing with Diesel, like a cat with a mouse.

And now it was going to eat him.

Peri drew his phaser and set it to 'Max'. He took careful aim, making sure he had a clean shot at the Crab's claw. He pulled the trigger and unleashed a long, sustained blast. 'Yes!' he said. He waited for the shell to crack or the monster to flail in pain, but nothing. The shot had had no effect. The creature's shell was just too strong and powerful.

Diesel was lowered towards the Crab's face. Peri lunged forward, determined not to let his friend be eaten!

He saw the creature's mouth for the first time. It was under the lip of the shell – a black, rectangular opening, like a trapdoor. It was easily big enough for Diesel.

Peri grabbed Diesel by the leg and tried to pull him away. He strained with all his might. Nothing happened. The Crab was far too strong.

Another claw pushed Peri away.

He could only watch in horror as Diesel got closer and closer to becoming space lunch for the Trojan Crab.

At the last moment, the claw veered away from the mouth. Instead, the Crab began to stuff Diesel under its shell, where

its cheek would be – if it had cheeks.
Diesel strained against the claw, trying
desperately to resist. But it was no good.
He disappeared into the shell. The Crab
pushed its claw underneath, poking him
further in. As if it was storing him in a
cupboard, to eat later.

Peri heard Diesel's anguished scream in
his earpiece. *'Aaaaaagh!'*

Then the scream trailed away. There was silence.

'Diesel?' Peri said. 'Can you hear me? Are you all right? Diesel?'

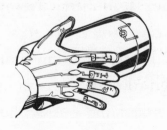

Chapter 5

Peri waited, feeling very small and alone, standing on the giant Trojan Crab in the silent emptiness of space.

After a few agonising moments Diesel's voice came through loud and clear. 'Hey! This is . . . weird.'

Peri felt a tingle of relief in his bionic circuits. 'You're alive! Where are you?'

'In some sort of weird place. It's like . . .'

'Have you found the Heart of Mars?' Peri asked.

'No. But you wouldn't believe how much

stuff there is in here, Peri. It's like . . . Aladdin's cave! You've got to see this!'

'Hold on,' Peri said. 'I'm coming in.'

He jetted towards the opening. A closed claw descended and pushed him away. He tried again, looking to swoop over the top of the claw and down behind it. But the Crab moved fast to bat him away once more. Peri went tumbling backwards, head over heels. Stars whirled round him.

'It won't let me in!' he complained, as he righted himself. 'How come it wants you and not me?'

He heard Diesel laugh. 'Maybe it's got good taste.'

'You'd better find the Heart of Mars and get out quick,' Peri said.

'I'm looking for it,' Diesel said. From inside the shell, Peri heard faint clattering sounds, as if junk was being moved around.

'But I dropped the Detector when I was pushed in here. Also — I don't know if I can get out.'

'What? Why not?'

'I'm trapped behind a mountain of weird shiny stuff. It's like —'

'Don't tell me,' Peri said. 'Aladdin's cave.'

He thought hard. He couldn't get in and Diesel couldn't get out. But why? They were both wearing Expedition Wear and looked the same — except that Diesel had that Martian flag draped over him . . .

Peri's brain went Superluminal.

The Crab had waved its claws around in time to the rays of his phaser. It had stuffed its shell full of glittering objects. It obviously liked bright, shiny things. Maybe it had been attracted by Diesel's colourful, shimmering cloak!

'Stay right where you are,' he told Diesel.

'I don't have much choice,' Diesel muttered.

Peri flipped the com-switch on his helmet to talk to the Bridge.

This time Selene answered. 'What's happening?' she asked. 'Where's Diesel?'

'We need to rescue him. Can you do something? In the ship's library there's a film about old Earth customs — *Did They Really Do That?* Can you access it through the computer and get the ship to transmit a holographic display of the section on fireworks? We want a really, *really* big display, OK?'

'I expect me and my dad can rig something up,' Selene said. 'What's it for?'

'It's to entertain a Trojan Crab,' Peri said.

Moments later, a huge fiery rocket soared through space. Then another, and another, until space seemed full of their fiery orange tails. A giant Catherine wheel burst into life, throwing out sparks of gold and silver. Red, yellow and green puffs of smoke erupted. A rain of twinkling diamonds fell.

The Crab's stalky eyes followed the display, mesmerised. Its claws slowly waved from side to side. If it could have spoken, Peri felt pretty sure it would be saying 'Oooh!' and 'Aaah!'

'I'm coming in!' Peri told Diesel.

He looked down at the safety cable that connected him to the *Phoenix*. He would need to take it off. The idea of being completely disconnected from the ship was scary, but he had no choice. He took a deep breath and unclipped the cable.

He zoomed towards the opening in the Crab's shell. This time, transfixed by the firework display, the creature made no attempt to stop him.

Peri dived into the blackness.

SQUELCH!

He had squished head first into a wall of something clingy and gloopy, like snot or uncooked egg white. It smelt a bit like rotten eggs too. Peri had to fight not to be sick.

Responding to the darkness, the lights on his Expedition Wear helmet came on. He saw that he was in some kind of viscous, green fluid.

He spoke into the com-unit. 'Diesel? I'm trapped in some sort of horrible snot!'

'Oh, yeah,' he heard Diesel say. 'You have to come through that.'

'Maybe you could have mentioned that before?' Peri said with a sigh.

'Sorry,' Diesel said. 'I got distracted by all the treasure in here. It's like –'

'Aladdin's cave,' Peri said. 'I know.' He hit

the control button of his rocket pack, going slow. For a few seconds he was completely surrounded by sticky, smelly green goo. He couldn't see anything. Then he emerged, with relief, on the other side. He wiped the gunge off his visor. He was in a sort of cosmic junkyard.

There were pieces of space debris — sections of old rockets, a tailpiece that Peri recognised from his history lessons at the IF Academy as part of *Sputnik* I, and a large silver hamburger, which was the familiar logo of Johnny Jupiter's Interstellar Hamburger Bar. He saw glittering chunks of quartz and other space-rocks that the Crab must have hoovered up on its travels. Peri gazed around, the light from his helmet illuminating objects as he turned. He saw the Elemental X-Ray Detector and pounced on it.

He scrambled over a huge piece of satellite telescope, aided by his rocket pack. On the other side, he saw Diesel sitting on an old aluminium bucket.

'About time,' Diesel said. 'I've been waiting ages.'

'Here,' Peri said, tossing him the Detector. 'Find the Heart of Mars.'

Diesel set it to 'Lead'. The Detector clicked as he passed it over the debris. The clicking grew louder and faster. 'We're close!' he said excitedly.

The clicking was loudest and fastest at the base of the satellite telescope. 'It must be under here,' Peri said. He slipped his fingers under the rim of the telescope and heaved. It toppled backwards and crashed into a heap of other space junk.

Peri grinned at the amazed expression on Diesel's face. 'There's hardly any gravity here,' he explained. 'The Crab is tiny compared to a planet, so objects weigh almost nothing. They still have the same mass though.'

'I was never good at physics,' Diesel said. 'It must be easy for you to understand, because you're half a robot.'

'I'm not half a robot, I'm *part* bionic!' Peri said. 'Anyway, weight depends on gravity. But even in zero gravity, a big dense object has the same mass – if it hit you, you'd be sorry.'

But Diesel wasn't listening. He gave a crow of delight as he leapt forward. He picked up a black lead cylinder and shook it. A heavy rattling came from inside! 'Found it!'

'Great!' said Peri. 'Now we can get out of here and go back to –'

He fell silent when he heard a scraping

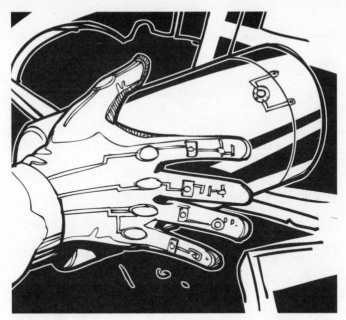

sound. Then a clinking. Then a rush like a metallic avalanche.

Peri spun round. The mountain of space junk he had crashed into was swaying. Its balance had been disturbed and it was falling towards the Crab's centre. There was enough mass there to crush Peri and Diesel like wafers.

And they were right in its path.

Chapter 6

Peri grabbed Diesel's arm and hit the rocket pack control. They jetted upwards. The avalanche of space junk was hurtling towards them. They'd be squashed flat if they didn't escape soon.

The top of the pile scraped their toes.

They'd only just cleared it.

Peri kept a tight hold of Diesel, who kept an even tighter hold on the Heart of Mars. With the rocket pack blaster on full, Peri towed his friend into the slime. He held his breath, trying not to breathe in the smell as the green goo clung to his visor again.

They finally emerged on the lip of the Crab's shell. Peri wiped his visor clean, relieved to see the infinite reaches of empty space.

The Crab was still watching the bright, sparkling lights of the firework display, its stalky eyes and its eight claws waving dreamily from side to side. It took no notice of Peri and Diesel.

'Let's have a look at that Heart of Mars,' Peri said.

Diesel clutched the cylinder to his chest. 'No chance! Only a Martian prince of the blood royal gets to look at the Heart!'

Peri sighed. 'OK. Well, let's get back to the ship.'

That was not going to be as easy as it sounded. The Trojan Crab was still whizzing through space at fifty kilometres a second. The *Phoenix*, though it looked motionless hanging there above them, was keeping pace. As soon as he and Diesel stepped off the Crab, they would be moving at fifty kilometres a second. If they were going in just slightly the wrong direction, the *Phoenix* would soon vanish into the far distance. The rocket pack would be nowhere near powerful enough to catch up.

'I'll call the others,' Peri said. 'They can teleport us aboard.' He flipped the com-switch in his helmet. 'Selene? Thanks for the firework display!'

'No problem,' Selene said. 'It was fun.'

'Can you get a fix on me and Diesel and —'

'Aaaarrggghmmmmf!' Selene screamed. 'Mmmmmfffff!'

'What?' Peri said. He could hear raised voices and clattering and . . . was that blaster fire in the background? 'Selene! Otto! Jaxx! What's happening?'

'Grrrummmmffffffff!' was all Selene said.

Then silence.

Diesel gasped. 'What's going on?'

Peri tried again to get through to the Bridge. This time there was no response at all.

'Something's wrong,' Peri said. 'It sounded like Selene was being attacked!'

'Attacked?'

'Why is no one answering now? I have a bad feeling about this.'

'So how do we get back on board the *Phoenix*?' demanded Diesel.

Peri spotted the end of his safety cable dangling not far behind them, but just out of reach. It was a gamble – but it looked like their only chance of getting back to the *Phoenix*.

'Hold on tight,' Peri said. 'I'm going to use the rocket pack to help us jump for the cable.'

'Are you crazy?' Diesel said. 'If we miss, the *Phoenix* will be on the other side of the galaxy within a second.'

'Do you have a better idea then?' Peri said.

Diesel said nothing. He just stood behind Peri and put one arm round his shoulders.

'No!' Peri said. 'You have to go in front, otherwise the rocket pack will scorch your legs off!'

Diesel moved in front of Peri and draped one arm round his neck.

'Why don't you hold on with both hands?' Peri asked.

'I'm not letting go of the Heart of Mars!'

Diesel said, clutching the lead cylinder to this chest.

'Well, you'd better not let go of me!' Peri said, as he stood on tiptoe on the very lip of the shell. This was going to take nerve, concentration and a very, very big leap.

He felt a tingling in his arms and legs. There was a surge of power within him. He could feel his strength increasing, his reflexes sharpening. His bionic powers were firing, at just the right moment!

'Let's do it,' Peri said.

He bent his knees and leapt into space with all his strength. At the same time he hit the 'Boost' button on the rocket pack control.

The safety cable came past at impossible speed.

Peri knew he had only one chance.

His outstretched hand *just* caught the cable.

He fumbled with the end of the safety cable, holding on with one hand, while he tried to attach it to the harness on his Expedition Wear. At last there was a click. 'Got it!'

Now they were safely attached and travelling at the same speed as the ship, Peri could use the rocket pack to speed up their progress.

They jetted towards the *Phoenix*. But then they started slowing down.

'What's happening?' demanded Diesel.

Peri glanced at the fuel gauge on the control. The needle pointed to zero. They must have used up all their fuel ploughing through the horrible snotty goo, and making their rocket-powered leap off the Trojan Crab.

'We'll have to haul ourselves up the cable,' Peri said.

Slowly, hand over hand, Peri pulled them both up. Diesel clung to Peri's neck with one arm, while his free hand clutched the lead cylinder.

He was no help at all.

For a long time, the silver egg shape of the *Phoenix* seemed to get no closer. Peri kept a slow and steady pace and soon they were nearly there.

Peri flicked the com-switch and called the Bridge again.

There was still no reply.

Peri knocked and called out: 'If anyone on the *Phoenix* can hear this, open the air-lock.'

Nothing happened.

Diesel growled with frustration. 'How are we going to get in?'

The sleek, gleaming underside of the *Phoenix* was right above them now. Peri reached out to touch it.

'It's no good stroking the hull!' Diesel said. He banged on the *Phoenix* with the lead cylinder. 'Let us in!'

'Hey, there's no need for that,' Peri said, feeling suddenly protective towards the vessel. 'Leave it alone. Let me see if I can –'

'What? What are you going to do?'

Peri's bionic side had a special connection to the *Phoenix*, an instinctive understanding of the ship's computer-brain. He laid his head against the smooth hull.

Can you hear me, Phoenix?

Deep inside, he felt a tingle in his bionic circuits that told him he had made contact with the ship.

Request permission to come aboard.

Again, he felt that tingling. He sensed the ship telling him: *Permission granted.*

Phoenix, Peri thought, *we need to be hidden from the sensors. It is very important to the safety of our friends.*

The air-lock slid silently open. Peri and Diesel hauled themselves on board.

'Wow!' Diesel said. 'What did you do?'

'We just had a little chat, me and the ship,' Peri said.

The outer door closed behind them. The air-lock flooded with oxygen. Arms shot from the walls and removed their Expedition Wear.

Peri felt a whisper in his mind. He screwed up his face in concentration as he listened to the *Phoenix*.

'What's wrong with your face?' Diesel asked.

'We have to go to the Bridge,' Peri said. 'Right now.'

Chapter 7

Peri and Diesel cautiously made their way along the silent corridors of the *Phoenix*, phasers in hand.

'What do you think's happened?' Diesel whispered.

'I don't know,' Peri whispered back. 'I only know there's some kind of danger. Maybe an intruder.'

They approached the Bridge. Peri touched the wall. It slid open. He and Diesel leapt in, holding their phasers out in front of them.

Jaxx was alone on the Bridge, standing by the control panel. He smiled. 'Hello. I trust the mission was a success?'

Peri and Diesel looked at each other in bewilderment. Jaxx seemed calm and relaxed. There was no evidence of any danger or any intruders.

'What happened?' Peri asked. 'Why didn't anyone answer when I tried to get through?'

'Sorry — we've been a little bit busy here,' Jaxx said.

'Busy doing what?' Diesel demanded.

'Oh, this and that,' Jaxx said casually. 'Did you get the Heart of Mars?'

'Yes,' Peri said. 'Eventually.'

'May I see it?' Jaxx held out his hand.

Diesel clutched the lead cylinder to his chest. 'No one touches this except me!'

Jaxx squared his shoulders. 'You'd better

hand it over,' he said, a hint of steel in his voice now.

'Hey,' Peri said as he noticed something else. 'Where are Selene and Otto?'

'They're safe,' Jaxx said, 'for now. However, they will be in great danger if you don't give me the Heart!'

'What are you saying?' Peri asked.

'You're not very bright for a Star Fighter, are you?' Jaxx said, shaking his head. 'I can see I'm going to have to spell this out in small words: Give. Me. The. Heart. Of. Mars. Or. Your. Two. Friends. Will . . .' His hand hovered over a touchpad on the control panel. 'Die. All I have to do is press this and they will be ejected into space. Ice-cold, pitch-dark, air-free space, where they will die in about, ooh, 3.5 seconds, I should say.'

Peri could not believe what he was

hearing. 'Are you crazy? How can you do this to your own daughter?'

Jaxx ignored him. He glared at Diesel. 'I don't like asking twice, Martian boy.'

Diesel held on tight to the cylinder. He shook his head. His strip of hair had turned black. 'You're not getting the Heart of Mars!' Diesel said. He raised his phaser and pointed it at Jaxx. 'I've set this to "Stuns" and "Really Hurts". Step away from the control panel.'

'Oh, that's a good idea,' Jaxx said brightly. 'Go on then. Zap me!'

'You asked for it!' Diesel pressed the firing button. Nothing happened except that the phaser gave out a low farting noise.

Jaxx clapped sarcastically. 'It didn't occur to you that I'd make Selene disable all on-board weapons systems, did it? Now,

I've had enough of messing around with you children.' He snapped his fingers. The other hand moved closer to the touchpad. 'Heart of Mars. Now.'

'Where are Selene and Otto?' Peri demanded. He was playing for time. 'We only have your word that you've got them. We're not trading the Heart for them until we know they're safe.'

Jaxx sighed. 'If you insist . . .'

He touched some buttons on the control panel. A second later, Selene and Otto materialised on the floor of the Bridge. They were kneeling on the the floor. Both were bound and gagged with Shrink-to-Fit Astro-Gaffer-Tape.

'Mmmmmfff!' said Selene.

'Ggggrmmmllfsh!' said Otto.

'Happy now?' Jaxx said.

'Selene!' Peri said. 'Are you OK?'

'She won't be OK,' Jaxx said, 'unless I get the Heart of Mars. So hand it over or else!'

Peri looked at Diesel. 'We have no choice,' he said.

For a few moments, Diesel was perfectly motionless. Peri felt an electric prickle in his chest. *Surely Diesel won't let Selene and Otto to die?* he thought. But then Diesel nodded and knelt down on the deck.

Peri breathed out in relief.

'No tricks, Martian boy,' Jaxx warned. 'You just stay where you are and roll that cylinder to me – nice and gently.'

Diesel rolled the cylinder to Jaxx.

'A wise decision,' Jaxx said and trapped the cylinder beneath his boot.

As Jaxx bent to pick it up, Diesel suddenly ran straight at the wall. He touched it, making it slide open to reveal the Emergency Escape Mini-Pod. This was a sort of space lifeboat, containing only a radio and enough oxygen to last twenty-four hours.

Diesel threw back the glass bubble roof and jumped in. The wall slid closed behind him. A moment later, the Mini-Pod was visible on the 360-monitor – a tiny white speck flying away from them.

What in space is Diesel doing? Peri wondered.

Jaxx raised his eyebrows. 'Strange boy,' he said. 'Well, he won't be missed. I have the Heart of Mars and that is all that matters!'

He unscrewed the lid of the cylinder and peeped inside.

Peri saw his forehead crease up in a puzzled frown.

Jaxx peered in more closely. He shook it. It made no sound.

Peri gasped in surprise.

What had happened to the Heart of Mars?

Jaxx turned the cylinder upside down. When nothing came out, his face crumpled – he looked like a little child who had just been stung by a Venusian flying jellyfish. He let out a wail so piercing that Peri had to put his hands over his ears. 'It's gone! *Gone!*'

Peri saw his chance. He beckoned to the

control panel and it glided over to him. He quickly re-enabled on-board weapons capabilities. His phaser gave a little bleep, indicating that it was operational once again.

He kept it trained on Jaxx as he pulled out the Bits and Bobs drawer from the wall. But Jaxx was showing no signs of hostility. He gazed into the empty lead cylinder, moaning to himself: 'I was so close . . . *So* close!'

Peri took out a pair of laser-scissors and cut through Selene's and Otto's bonds. They both sat up and peeled away their gags, wincing and gasping for air.

'Are you OK?' Peri asked them.

Otto growled, extending his snake-like neck in Jaxx's direction.

'Easy,' Peri said. 'Maybe something happened to him. Maybe he's gone temporarily insane.'

'No, he's always like this!' Selene said.

Peri realised that she had not jumped to her dad's defence as she normally would have done. Instead she was staring at him with hatred.

She ran to Jaxx and gripped his collar with both hands. 'What have you done with my dad?' she shouted.

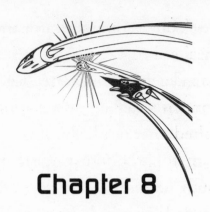

Chapter 8

'Selene,' Jaxx said, 'you need to calm yourself. Maybe a little lie-down would do you good.'

He gave Selene a violent shove and sent her sprawling across the floor.

Peri felt a surge of anger. He pointed his phaser at Jaxx. 'You leave her alone!'

'Yes, I will,' Jaxx said. He seemed to have got over his disappointment and was his cool, collected self again. 'As long as she leaves *me* alone. Now, excuse me – I have a call to make.'

He took out a communicator and flipped it open.

Peri ran to help Selene to her feet. 'Are you hurt?' he asked.

She shook her head. 'I'm fine –'

'She may not be hurt,' Otto bellowed, 'but someone soon *will* be!'

'Captain Flintbeard,' Jaxx said into the communicator, 'I want you to – *errrfff!*'

Otto had charged forward and knocked him flat on his back. Otto sat astride him, his knees pinning Jaxx's arms to the floor. 'Got you! You're heading straight to an IF prison!'

Peri looked at Selene, confused. 'Let me get this straight. Jaxx – your dad – *is* the space pirate?'

'No,' Selene shook her head. 'But *he* is.' She pointed to Jaxx.

Now Peri shook his head in complete

and utter confusion. Had Selene lost her mind? 'What? That is Jaxx.'

'No, his name is Daxx,' Selene said.

'Now I'm really confused,' Peri said.

Selene's voice was a snarl that Peri had never heard her make before. 'He's my dad's identical twin,' she said. 'My uncle.'

'But – what happened to your dad then?' Peri asked.

'Daxx beamed himself aboard while you were down on the Trojan Crab, and beamed Jaxx off!' She knelt and shouted into Daxx's face. 'What have you done with my dad?'

'If you want to see him again,' Daxx said, 'tell this Meigwor maniac to get off me.'

Selene hesitated. Then she tapped Otto on the shoulder. 'You'd better get off him.'

'Can't I just rough him up a bit first?' Otto said.

Selene cocked her head as if she was

considering it. 'He deserves it,' she said, 'but I don't think it would help me get my dad back.'

Otto reluctantly stood up. Daxx got to his feet, dusting himself off.

'Sooooo,' Peri said, drawing the word out. 'You're the evil twin.'

'I prefer to think of myself as the *smart* twin,' Daxx said with a smirk. He picked up the fallen communicator. 'Captain Flintbeard, sorry for the interruption. Uncloak the *Space Wolf*, would you?'

'What about my dad?' demanded Selene.

Daxx sneered at her. 'Patience, please, my dear niece.'

'What's the *Space Wolf*?' Peri asked.

Daxx pointed to the 360-monitor. A spaceship was gradually becoming visible. It had masts and silver sails like an ancient galleon. A white flag flew from the tallest mast. It had a strange image of a skull-and-crossed-swords. Peri knew from old Earth movies about sea pirates that this type of flag was called a 'Jolly Roger'. Space pirates called them a 'Cranky Roger'.

'That's the *Space Wolf*,' Daxx said. 'Isn't she a beauty?'

'Is that where my dad is?'

Daxx waved at Selene to be quiet. 'Captain Flintbeard, an escape-pod was ejected from the *Phoenix* about a minute ago. Send out a Stealth Snapper to track it down and capture it. But don't destroy the pod. There's something on board that I need.' Daxx listened for a moment. 'No, of course it doesn't matter if you kill the pilot!'

Peri felt a jolt of horror. Diesel was arrogant and spoilt and there was no denying he could be a cosmic pain in the neck. But he was still a comrade. Peri had to help him out — somehow.

On the 360-monitor, he saw a small craft emerge from the belly of the *Space Wolf*. It was black, with a pointed snout. It had no masts, no sails and no flag, but a Cranky Roger was painted on the side. It shot off in the direction that Diesel's mini-pod had been heading.

Peri felt his pulse quicken with dread. Mini-pods weren't designed for speed. The Stealth Snapper would catch Diesel in a matter of minutes.

Peri pulled the control panel to him. He opened the ship's Power System and deftly programmed it to give a massive charge of extra power to one of the remaining mini-pods.

'What are you doing there?' Daxx demanded.

Peri didn't answer. He simply thought the words *Super-charged mini-pod*. Then he headed for the wall of the Bridge. The wall opened silently and there was the pod, its roof already lifted.

'Oh no you don't!' snapped Daxx as he lunged for Peri.

Otto's long crimson arm shot out, caught Daxx around the waist and flung him to the floor. 'Oh no *you* don't!' the Meigwor boomed.

Peri didn't stay to watch what happened next. He jumped into the mini-pod. The roof closed over him as an astro-harness clicked into place. He pulled the twin thrust-levers and the mini-pod zoomed away from the *Phoenix*, into outer space.

The g-force slammed Peri back into his seat. The mini-pod was definitely charged up!

'Diesel?' Peri said into the com-unit. 'I'm coming after you.'

'Don't try to bring me back!' Diesel said. 'I have to keep the Heart of Mars safe. I've called the Martian Imperial Fleet to come and pick me up.'

'They'll never get there in time,' Peri said. 'There's a pirate stealth ship after you!'

'Kriimb' la-kooshwoggle!'

'Take evasive action for as long as you can,' Peri said. 'I'm coming to help!'

The mini-pod roared silently through space. Ahead, Peri saw the Stealth Snapper. The Proximeter on the instrument panel told him it was only a hundred kilometres away. At this speed, that was almost touching distance.

A moment later, Peri saw Diesel's mini-pod. The Snapper was almost on it. 'Dodge!' he shouted into the radio.

A nanosecond later, Diesel's pod veered sharply, just as a bright yellow ball appeared where he'd only just been flying.

Peri was impressed with Diesel's piloting skills. But he was also worried – because the Snapper was firing Incinerator Balls.

The IF had outlawed Incinerator Balls as weapons over a hundred years earlier. They were super-hot clouds of blazing hydrogen that briefly enveloped a target. They burned and died out in a nanosecond. They would not destroy a ship, but anybody inside would be fried.

Peri lined the Snapper up in his laser cannon sights and fired.

A blinding white ray shot through space and clipped the side of the Snapper.

Now it knows I'm here, Peri thought.

He was already tugging on the Nav-wheel as the Snapper swung round and fired back

at him. The mini-pod rocketed above the Incinerator Ball, then he saw it explode below him and felt a wave of heat.

In the middle distance Peri saw a silver-blue sphere hanging motionless in space. It was Io, one of Jupiter's moons. He would have to be careful not to get too close, or its gravitational pull would suck him towards it.

The Snapper turned back to Diesel's pod and fired another Incinerator Ball. This one came close enough to knock Diesel off course and send his pod spinning towards Io.

The Snapper re-aligned so that its weapon could track Diesel. It was getting ready for a final, decisive and deadly strike.

Before it could fire, Peri blasted his laser cannon again.

This time the white ray found its mark.

The Stealth Snapper lit up, its colours reversed for an instant – its black hull turned white, and its white Cranky Roger turned black. Then it went careering off course. Peri breathed a sigh of relief.

He radioed Diesel. 'Are you OK?'

'I can't break free of Io's gravity,' Diesel said in between cries of fear. 'I'm going to have to crash-land!'

Peri hoped the mini-pod's boosters would

be powerful enough to slow its descent. Otherwise it would smash up on impact.

He heard an ominous bleeping noise and glanced at his radar screen. Three dots were heading his way, fast.

He looked back out into space and saw three Stealth Snappers bearing down on him.

Chapter 9

The three Snappers fired a volley of Incinerator Balls. Peri dived under the first one and steered the mini-pod in between the other two. He looped-the-loop and fired his laser cannon, forcing the Snappers to swerve.

He braced himself for them to return to the attack. But they didn't. They turned away from him and dived towards Io.

Of course! Peri thought. *They're not going to waste time on me. They want Diesel. They want the Heart of Mars.*

He radioed the *Phoenix*. With relief, he heard Selene's voice. 'Is that you, Peri?'

'Yes,' he told her. 'Diesel has landed on Io. The space pirates are after him. Can you get a fix on his pod and teleport him aboard the *Phoenix*?'

'Sure.'

'Can you do it without Daxx knowing?'

'Sure.' Selene chuckled. 'Otto's taking care of my uncle.'

'Diesel may have landed with quite a bump,' Peri said. 'Beam him up to the Med Centre.'

Peri turned towards the *Phoenix*. The super-charged pod took him back in no time.

The outer wall of the *Phoenix* slid open. Peri docked. The air-lock closed behind him. Peri jumped from the pod and ran along the smooth, mauve-lit corridors

until he reached a portal. *Med Centre*, he thought. The door hissed open.

Peri's parents had upgraded the Med Centre when the ship was refitted, and it had been designed to make patients feel more comfortable. A Levi-bed floated by the wall. Soft, plinky-plonky xylophone music played through speakers that Peri couldn't see. A fountain burbled in one corner. The Android Doctor stood silently in another corner, waiting to be activated. It was a calm and relaxing environment. But Peri did not feel calm or relaxed.

Where is Diesel?

A shimmering patch appeared on the Levi-bed.

'No – go away!' Peri heard Diesel's angry voice shout. 'You can't have the Heart of Mars!'

As Peri watched, the shimmering patch materialised into Diesel. He had a bruise on his cheek and a cut on his hand.

He stopped shouting when he saw Peri. He looked momentarily confused, then broke into a broad grin. 'Oh, it's just you. Those space pirates were just about to break into my pod –'

'Well, you're safe now,' Peri said. 'Are you OK?'

The Android Doctor's eyes flashed blue.

It moved forward on noiseless wheels and bent to examine Diesel. *'Hmm, what seems to be the trouble?'* it said. *'Looks like some minor cuts and bruises to me. Nothing to worry about, young man.'* It dabbed antiseptic cream on Diesel's hand and gave him two white pills. *'Take these if you feel any pain. Call me in the morning if you don't improve!'*

It reversed back into the corner and the light went out of its eyes.

Peri helped Diesel to his feet. 'Have you got the Heart of Mars?'

Diesel nodded. He patted his pocket. 'But anyone who wants it is going to have to kill me first!'

'But it's not just *your* life that's in danger,' Peri pointed out. 'You were prepared to let Selene and Otto die to save it.'

'You don't understand,' Diesel said. 'It has to be saved at all costs!'

'Why? Come on, you don't really believe that all Martians will be cursed. It must be something else.'

Diesel shook his head. 'I'm not allowed to say.'

'Diesel, you have to help us here. Daxx has got Jaxx and —'

'Daxx has got Jaxx? What does that mean?'

Peri realised that Diesel wasn't up to speed. 'The guy on the Bridge is not Selene's dad. He's his twin brother, Daxx. He's holding the real Jaxx hostage until we hand over the Heart of Mars.'

'So? That's not my problem.'

Peri looked at him steadily. 'It's a big problem for Selene — and she's our comrade. If Daxx doesn't get the Heart of Mars, she'll never see her dad again. Those space pirates will probably kill him. What's more important – saving a human life, or saving the Heart of Mars?'

'Saving the Heart of Mars!' Diesel said immediately.

'Come on, Diesel!' Peri said. 'It was Selene who saved *you* just now, you know? It was her who beamed you off Io in the nick of time. The least you can do is help save her dad.'

Diesel chewed his lip.

'Don't forget we're on a mission from the IF!' Peri said. 'Now that we know Daxx is the *real* pirate, it's our duty to arrest him.'

'Arrest him, yes,' Diesel said. 'I'm fine with that. But not with giving him the Heart.' He patted his pocket protectively.

'We need to bargain with him to get him to release Jaxx,' Peri explained. '*Then* we can arrest him and get the Heart of Mars back.'

The strip of hair on Diesel's head went

through a whole spectrum of colours, as if he was thinking hard. 'So you mean, just . . . *show* it to him?'

'Well, sort of. We might have to let him hold it. But once we've got Jaxx back —'

'Then we double-cross him!'

'Yeah,' Peri said. 'Sort of.'

He didn't think it was a *real* double-cross. The agreement was to exchange the gemstone for Jaxx, and that was exactly what they were going to do. *After* the exchange had been made, however, the fact remained that Daxx was still a space pirate in possession of stolen property and they were entitled to get it back from him. But if Diesel preferred to see it as a double-cross, Peri wasn't going to argue.

Diesel nodded reluctantly. 'Oh . . . all right then.'

'Let's get to the Bridge!' Peri said.

The first thing Peri saw was Otto sitting on Daxx's chest.

'Get off me, you disgusting entity!' Daxx said.

'I am not disgusting,' Otto said, picking his nose and placing an ultra-large Meigwor bogey on the end of his tongue. 'And you should learn some manners!'

'Hi, guys!' Peri said.

Daxx twisted his head to look at Diesel. He groaned. 'Those stupid incompetent pirates! They let you get away!'

'You all right, Diesel?' Selene said.

Diesel looked at the ground. Peri thought he might have blushed. 'Yeah. Er – thanks.'

'We need to talk,' Peri said. 'Otto, you can get off Daxx now.'

'*Oof!*' Daxx said, as Otto's weight was lifted from his chest.

'Here's the situation,' Peri said. 'Daxx,

you have Selene's dad. We have the Heart of Mars! Show him, Diesel.'

Slowly, Diesel put his hand in his pocket and drew out the precious stone.

Peri caught his breath. The Heart of Mars was the size of a large peach. It glowed with a warm orange light, as if it was alive. As Diesel turned it in his hand, something seemed to be moving in its depths, and sparkles and rays of orange, yellow, silver and gold light darted from it. It made everything else on the Bridge look dull. Nobody could look at anything else.

'Wow,' Selene said softly.

'Do you want to trade?' Peri said to Daxx. 'The Heart of Mars for our friend's dad?'

Daxx licked his lips. 'Do you really need an answer to that?'

Otto waved his double-jointed arms at Peri. 'This is wrong! Our job is to *arrest*

space pirates, not give them precious stones!'

'We have no choice,' Peri said. 'Daxx, get ready to beam your brother aboard. The moment he materialises, you get the Heart of Mars. That's the deal.'

Then Peri saw Diesel backing away, gazing at the Heart of Mars. He slipped the stone back into his pocket and the light seemed to go out of the room.

Peri felt a sickening sense of dread. 'Diesel, what are you playing at?'

'I won't give it away!' Diesel said. His face looked grimly defiant. 'I can't. If you want it, you'll have to kill me.'

Chapter 10

'Diesel!' Peri said. 'You agreed!'

Diesel's strip of hair had turned an angry red. 'I've changed my mind!'

Peri saw Selene reach into the pocket of her overalls. 'Hey, Diesel?' she said.

Diesel turned his face to look at her. 'What?'

'Catch!'

Selene tossed a yellow-and-green ball with rubbery tendrils to Diesel. He instinctively caught it. The rubbery tendrils stuck to his hands and the ball started buzzing.

'*Ch'ach!* What —'

A smile spread over his face. He started laughing uncontrollably. He bent double, then slid helplessly to the floor, snorting with laughter like a Shantanian warthog.

'What in space was that?' Peri asked.

'Hilaro-Ball,' Selene said, with a grin. 'Me and my dad invented it together. It tickles the pleasure nerves and sends you into fits of laughter. But it doesn't last long — so we'd better move fast!'

She plucked the Heart of Mars from Diesel's pocket.

'All right, Uncle Daxx,' she said, holding the precious stone out for him to see. 'Get ready to beam my dad aboard. As soon as I see he's unharmed, I throw this to you.'

Daxx pointed a finger at her, his face stern. 'And if you don't throw it to me, I send him straight back — right?'

Selene nodded. 'Right.'

'I'll count to three,' Peri said. A plan was forming in his mind. As soon as the swap was made, he would dive for the control panel and hit the touchpad that controlled the Exo-Zoological Specimen Container, trapping Daxx in an unbreakable transparent cylinder. 'One . . . Two . . . Three!'

Daxx hit the teleportation button.

A shimmering patch of light appeared on the Bridge. It materialised into Jaxx. He blinked, looking around him in surprise.

'Are you all right, Dad?' Selene asked.

Jaxx rubbed his head, which Peri guessed had been made sore by the pirates. 'I think so.'

Selene threw the Heart of Mars to Daxx, who caught it one-handed.

'What was that?' Jaxx said. He sounded alarmed. 'You haven't given him —'

Peri hurled himself at the control panel.

Daxx slammed his free hand down on to a button.

Peri rose into the air and flew right past him. He didn't stop until he hit the far wall of the Bridge and bounced off.

Twisting around, he saw Selene, Otto, Jaxx and Diesel all floating helplessly in the air.

Daxx's feet were planted firmly on the floor.

'What have you done?' Otto shouted.

'Didn't I tell you I'm the smart twin?' Daxx said. 'I just disabled the *Phoenix*'s artificial gravity, that's all. No problem if you're wearing the right footwear, of course!'

He did a couple of gliding dance steps. Peri saw that he was wearing magnetised spacewalk shoes.

Diesel was still laughing, even as he slowly spun in the air.

'This isn't funny!' Jaxx said to him. 'You don't realise how serious –'

'Yes I do!' said Diesel, in between snorts of laughter. 'It's a total disaster!'

Peri frantically beckoned to the control panel. It started to move towards him. Then Daxx intercepted it and tied the astro-harness of the pilot's seat around it.

The control panel strained at the harness like a dog on a lead.

'Time for my exit line, I think,' Daxx said. He waved at them. 'So long, suckers!'

'Don't be stupid, brother!' Jaxx said. 'You can't get away with this! Give yourself up to the IF authorities.'

'Let me see,' Daxx said, stroking his chin. 'Get locked up in prison, or get clean away with the Heart of Mars? It's a tough one, but I think I've made my decision.'

He took out his communicator and flipped it open. 'Can you get a fix on me? I'm on the Bridge of the *Phoenix*. Beam me on board the *Space Wolf* as soon as you can!'

Peri managed to twist round and aim his phaser at Daxx.

Daxx looked horrified. He raised his hands. 'Please, don't shoot!'

Peri pulled the trigger.

The phaser made a low, farting noise.

An electric surge of pure frustration flowed through Peri's circuits.

Daxx smirked. 'Did you really imagine I wouldn't have thought of that?'

'We have to stop him!' Jaxx said. He began to swim through the air towards his brother.

Diesel was nearer to Daxx. Still giggling, he made a desperate lunge and grabbed hold of Daxx's wrist.

'Get off!' Daxx said.

'Drop the Heart of Mars, wastoid!' Diesel laughed.

Daxx's body began to shimmer. 'The Heart of Mars is coming with me. If you choose to come too, that will be your funeral. Literally!'

Diesel's body began to shimmer and fade like Daxx's.

'Let go, Diesel!' Peri shouted.

Diesel was desperately trying to prise Daxx's hand open. 'I can't!'

'If you don't,' Peri called, 'you'll be teleported on to the pirate ship with him!'

'I can't lose the Heart of Mars —'

'Let go, Diesel!' shouted Peri, Selene, Otto and Jaxx all together.

Peri summoned his bionic power, kicked off against the ceiling and sailed straight for his friend. He peeled Diesel's hand from Daxx, finger by finger, and jerked him free. Diesel screamed as if he was in agony.

'Hang loose, guys!' Daxx said and disappeared.

'You don't know what you've done?' Diesel cried.

'I saved your life,' Peri said and shoved Diesel away from him.

'What do I press?' Otto said. He had used his long arms to pull himself within range of the control panel.

'The grey button!' Peri said.

Gravity was restored. They all hit the ground, with five simultaneous bumps.

'*Aaaaaagh!*' screamed Diesel again. He was not laughing any more. 'You total dumb-oids. You've just given away the Heart of Mars!'

'I know it was a beautiful stone,' Peri said. 'But it's still only a stone. You don't believe in the curse, do you?'

'It's worse than a curse,' Diesel said. 'Worse than you could ever know!'

'What do you mean?' Selene demanded.

Diesel scowled. 'I won't tell you! I made a solemn promise to the emperor that I would never reveal its true powers!'

'What true powers?' Otto boomed.

Diesel's mouth shut in a stubborn line.

'I think I have an idea what he means,' Jaxx said slowly. His face was pale and his forehead was furrowed. 'On the *Space Wolf*, I heard the pirates talking.'

'What did they say, Dad?' Selene asked, looking as worried as Peri felt.

'The Heart of Mars is an awesome source of energy. They plan to use it as the final element in a weapon so deadly that it could destroy the whole Milky Way.'

There was a long silence.

Peri felt sick. He blamed himself. Diesel had told him the Heart of Mars had to be saved at all costs – and he hadn't believed it.

'Does anyone want to say sorry to me?' Diesel demanded.

'Don't blame me!' Otto boomed. 'I said we shouldn't let the space pirate have it!'

Peri put his hand on Diesel's shoulder. 'We'll get it back.'

'We'll get it back!' echoed Selene.

'We *have* to get it back,' Jaxx said grimly.

'But how?' Diesel wailed.

Peri sat at the Nav-wheel. His astro-harness snapped around him. On the 360-monitor, he could see a tiny dot flying away from them. He zoomed in on the image and the *Space Wolf* came into view – with its masts and solar-wind sails and its Cranky Roger.

'Follow that pirate ship!' he said as he jammed the thrusters to 'Max'.

Can Peri and the crew get the Heart of Mars back and save the Milky Way?

Will they make it through the deadly booby traps in the Astro-Void?

Find out! In ...

Turn over to read Chapter 1

Chapter 1

'Daxx is escaping!' Peri shouted as the *Space Wolf* blazed away from the *Phoenix*.

The space pirates' vessel had every solar-wind sail unfurled like an ancient galleon. The skull-and-crossed-swords flag, the Cranky Roger, streamed behind the ship. Daxx had stolen the Heart of Mars and planned to use it in a secret weapon that could threaten the entire galaxy. It was the Star Fighters' mission to get the priceless gem back.

Peri smacked on the emergency boosters. 'We need more speed!' he shouted.

The g-force knocked Diesel to the floor as the *Phoenix* surged forward, but the half-Martian scrambled up and pushed past Otto to reach the gunnery station.

'Where's Jaxx?' Peri asked, scanning the Bridge.

Jaxx was the IF's Space Enemy Number One. They had captured him when he had nearly crash-landed on Saturn only to find out he was Selene's father. She was sure he was innocent, and that his identical twin brother, Daxx, was the real space pirate.

'I sent my dad to Engineering to try and improve the plasma flow to the thrusters,' Selene said, checking over the engineer's console. 'If anyone can make us go faster, my dad can!'

Without warning, Daxx's ship plunged towards a fiery red dwarf star.

'What on Mars is he doing?' Peri said, twisting the Nav-wheel and diving after the *Space Wolf*.

'Perhaps he's using the star's gravity field to slow us down,' Diesel suggested.

Gravity! The word lit up a bionic circuit in Peri's head. 'No, he's going to use the gravity field like a slingshot, to catapult his ship even faster out the other side of the star.'

The gauges on the control panel went haywire as they got closer to the star. The *Phoenix* began to shake. Peri knew their ship would be pulled apart and they'd be burnt alive if they got too close. But if they were too far away, they wouldn't be able to swing round the star fast enough to catch up with Daxx.

Peri watched as the space pirates' ship caught the gravitational pull of the dwarf star and zoomed away. Daxx had timed it perfectly. Now it was Peri's turn. He gripped the Nav-wheel and yanked the thrusters to 'Max'.

Shhhwooosh! The *Phoenix* whipped round the dying star. It shot them after Daxx's ship at astonishing speed. They hurtled through entire solar systems in the blink of an eye, right on the space pirates' tail.

Fsssssshhhhwooor! They skimmed past a planet, narrowly missing two moons.

'*Dung y'r'ah!*' Diesel gasped. 'That was cosmic-close!'

Peri dodged left and right, copying Daxx's moves. His brain buzzed with excitement. It wouldn't be long before Daxx would have to stop — then they would swoop down and bring him to justice.

Narrrooa! They slipped past comets and asteroids.

Suddenly, Daxx zigzagged and whipped sharply to the right.

'He's making evasive manoeuvres!' Peri yelled as the *Phoenix* zipped past Daxx's ship and watched it vanish into clouds of yellow-grey space-fog.

Peri slammed on the turbo-reverse. Instantly, the *Phoenix* spun round and shot into the cloud after Daxx. A thick mist folded around the ship.

'I'm tracking him on the Velocity View,' said Peri.

'I love a good chase!' Otto boomed. The Meigwor bounty hunter paced the Bridge excitedly.

'Does Daxx know we're following him?' Diesel asked.

'Dad and I made sure the *Phoenix*'s cloak is set at one hundred per cent efficiency,' Selene said. 'The *Space Wolf* doesn't have powerful enough sensors to detect us.'

The Bridge lights dimmed and glowed

red. '*Cosmic turbulence ahead,*' announced the calm voice of the ship's computer.

An astro-harness snaked around Peri. His stomach lurched as the *Phoenix* plunged into a patch of turbulence. The floating control panel flipped away from his grasp. Peri grabbed it with his fingertips and hauled it back as the *Phoenix* was buffeted by the space-fog.

'*Frrr'wowoh!*' Otto screamed as he was thrown into the air, bounced against the ceiling and then slammed against the deck. '*Oooph!*' The Meigwor used his long arms to grab hold of the control panel. He stared at Peri. 'Blast the space pirates! Then we can get out of here!'

'No!' Diesel cried. 'We need the Heart of Mars in one piece to lift the curse on my planet.'

'Who cares about that stupid jewel?' Selene

snapped. 'I need Daxx alive to clear my dad's name. The IF needs proof that it's Daxx who's the real space pirate!'

'Hold on tight!' Peri yelled as the *Phoenix* burst from the nebula cloud. They were only seconds behind Daxx, but their target had changed direction again. He was swerving around the wreck of a plasma-tanker. Peri dodged between the corroded metal ribs of the tanker's hull and shot out the other side. *We're catching him!*

Red lights flashed across the control panel, but it wasn't another space-hazard. It was something potentially worse – an incoming message from the IF Command Centre.

'Otto, Selene – hide!' Peri shouted. The IF didn't know anything about Otto and Selene being aboard the *Phoenix*. If they did, Peri and Diesel would be in serious galactic trouble.

Otto raced across the Bridge and slid behind the gunnery station, but Selene wasn't as fast. Diesel pushed her to the floor.

'Lie flat and keep quiet,' the half-Martian hissed as the 360-monitor whirled up, showing the tired face of General Pegg.

'I will not keep quiet!' The general glared at Diesel. 'Star Fighters – report on your mission progress,' he barked.

'Sir –' Peri started.

'I've checked your Mission Capsule coord-inates,' the general interrupted. 'Your objective was to capture Jaxx. What are you doing on that side of the universe?'

'We're hot on the heels of the pirate who stole the Heart of Mars,' Peri replied.

The general took a sharp breath. 'I hope you know what you're doing. You're head-ing straight for an Astro-Void.'

Peri frowned. Apart from Daxx's ship,

there was nothing at all on the 360-monitor in front of them. Peri wondered what the general was talking about. 'Sir?'

'An Astro-Void, Peri,' the general snapped. 'Diesel, you took astro-navigation classes – explain it to him.'

'I got top marks in my class, but I don't think we covered . . .'. Diesel looked at Peri for support, but Peri just shrugged.

There was a tiny cough from below and they both looked down. Silently Selene put her hands together, then opened them out as wide as she could.

Diesel shook his head. 'What the *prrrip'chiq* does that mean?' the gunner muttered.

Selene rolled her eyes. 'It's a vast dark space between galaxies,' she whispered.

'What's going on?' General Pegg's eyes bulged. 'Who else is on your ship?'

Peri's throat tightened. General Pegg was

going to confiscate their Star Fighter badges for hiding Selene on board, but they couldn't pretend she wasn't there now. Peri reached down and helped her stand up. 'Selene is –'

'I know who she is! She's a stowaway and a troublemaker,' the general snapped. 'I've kicked her off the IF Space Station more times than I can remember, yet somehow she always manages to return.'

Selene shrugged. 'It's not my fault that

your security systems don't work properly.'

'Quiet!' General Pegg ordered. 'I will not have civilians on an official IF mission. Lock Selene in a holding cell for her own safety – and yours. Return with her and that space pirate in custody soon, or your Star Fighter careers will be the shortest in IF history! End message.'

Peri felt stunned as the 360-monitor whirled back into the control panel. Why hadn't he explained to General Pegg that Selene was an incredible engineer and a valuable member of the crew? They couldn't afford to lose her from the *Phoenix*.

Diesel pulled out a pair of handcuffs. 'Are you going to come along quietly then?' he asked Selene.

Selene leapt back. 'You spineless creep! After all I've done to save you!'

Diesel's yellow eyes flashed. 'No one

has ever needed to save *me*, you bossy bugonaut!'

Peri jumped up and put himself between them. 'No one is arresting Selene. Diesel, give me the cuffs.'

Diesel's narrow band of hair bristled as he handed them over. 'I can't believe you're taking her side.'

'She's part of the crew,' Peri said. 'End of story.'

'Hey, Earthlings!' Otto boomed, crawling out from behind the gunnery station. 'The cosmic-rat has led us to his nest!'

Peri turned to look where Otto was pointing. The 360-monitor showed that Daxx's vessel was heading straight for a huge shimmering blue planet.

Selene hit the intercom switch and shouted, 'Dad, come to the Bridge! You've got to see this.' Then she slammed the

'Emergency Stop' button, making the *Phoenix* come to a dead stop.

'What are you doing?' Peri demanded.

Selene put her hands on her hips. 'I don't understand. There shouldn't be any planets in an Astro-Void.'

Jaxx materialised next to Selene. He started activating the scanners.

They watched Daxx's ship duck and swerve on its approach to the shimmering blue planet as if it was flying an obstacle course.

Then the *Space Wolf* disappeared.

'He's just vanished like a plasma-phantom!' Jaxx exclaimed. 'There's no sign of cloak activation, not even a heat signature.'

Peri realised that something was horribly wrong.